08~ BRe- 222

# Winter Pony

# Winter Pony

By Jean Slaughter Doty

Illustrated by Ruth Sanderson

**A STEPPING STONE BOOK™**
Random House New York

Text copyright © 1975 by Jean Slaughter Doty
Illustrations copyright © 2008 by Ruth Sanderson

Published in the United States by Random House Children's Books,
a division of Random House, Inc., New York. Originally published by
The Macmillan Company in slightly different form in 1975.

Random House and colophon are registered trademarks and
A Stepping Stone Book and colophon are trademarks of
Random House, Inc.

Visit us on the Web!
www.steppingstonesbooks.com
www.randomhouse.com/kids

Educators and librarians, for a variety of teaching tools, visit us at
www.randomhouse.com/teachers

*Library of Congress Cataloging-in-Publication Data*
Doty, Jean Slaughter, 1924–1991.
Winter pony / by Jean Slaughter Doty ; illustrated by Ruth Sanderson.
    p.   cm.
"Stepping Stone book."
Summary: In this sequel to Summer Pony, Ginny now owns Mokey
and assists her in giving birth to a beautiful foal.
ISBN 978-0-375-84710-3 (trade) — ISBN 978-0-375-94710-0 (lib. bdg.)
[1. Ponies—Fiction.]  I. Sanderson, Ruth, ill. II. Title.
PZ10.3.D7197Wi 2008
[Fic]—dc22   2007019091

Printed in the United States of America

10  9  8  7  6  5  4  3  2  1

First Edition

*To Black Jack—*
*who loved the snow and the sound of the bells*
*—J.S.D.*

*For Whitney*
*—R.S.*

# Chapter One

"Hey, Mokey!" Ginny Anderson ran down the hill. She called cheerfully to her pony. A small bucket of hot mash swung from her hand.

Mokey whinnied in answer. Ginny could hear her through the twilight. Ginny could also hear the sound of quick hoofbeats. She saw Mokey in a blurred pattern of brown and white. Mokey trotted up to the paddock gate.

"Hi, Moke." Ginny stopped to give her pony a quick pat. Then she let herself into the small tack room. It was in the stable, next to the paddock. She turned on the lights and un-hooked the narrow door into the stall. Mokey was waiting inside. She was peering into her

feed tub. She looked like she was waiting for her supper to appear like magic. Ginny poured the sweet hot mash into the tub. Mokey stuck her muzzle deep into the swirling steam with a sigh of joy.

Ginny left the pony to enjoy her supper in peace. Ginny went to stand for a moment by the open stall door. It led to the paddock next door.

The frosty twilight sky was turning purple. The evening star glowed brightly over a far ridge of trees.

"Star light, star bright," said Ginny. She stopped. There was no need to go on. For years she had wished on every star, ever since she could remember, for a pony of her own. Now she had Mokey, with her brown and white spots, her one blue eye and one brown, her black forelock and white mane and black tail. Mokey was not exactly the beautiful pony of her dreams. But she was a real, live pony.

Mokey was fat now and shaggy. Her winter coat was getting thicker. The new little stable had just been finished. It was painted a deep red with white trim. It smelled like fresh sawdust, drying paint, sweet hay, and pony.

Ginny squinted up at the evening star. It seemed hard to remember how thin and shabby Mokey had been just last spring. She and her mother had found the pony at the Sweetbriar Pony Farm. They rented her just for the summer. But the whole family had become so fond of the pony that they couldn't let her go when the summer ended.

It was getting colder. Ginny shivered. She went outside to close the heavy Dutch doors of the stall to shut Mokey in for the night.

Mokey finished her mash. She slobbered a last happy mouthful over the front of Ginny's jacket. Then she turned to start on her hay. Ginny finished cleaning the stall. She added fresh bedding and filled the water bucket to the brim. The weather report said there would be a hard frost that night. Ginny brought out Mokey's new winter blanket and buckled it on.

"You greedy thing," Ginny said to her pony. "This blanket fit just right when we got it for you. Now I have to loosen the back belt buckle. You're getting fatter every day."

Ginny smoothed the pony's mane. She gave her a loving pat.

"Tomorrow is Saturday," Ginny said. "We can be out all day. And you sure need the exercise to work off some of that tummy!"

Ginny bolted the narrow door behind her as she left the stall. She stood for a happy moment in the tack room. She checked to see that everything was in its place. Bales of hay and shavings for bedding were neatly stacked at the back of the room. The ceiling lights glowed on the dark leather of the halter and bridle. They were on their racks on the wall. Ginny could see the white cotton lead ropes. The buckets and metal storage cans for grain were under the shelf where the brushes and grooming things were kept. The pitchfork, rake, and broom were hung on the wall where they belonged. Ginny was humming softly under her breath. She turned off the lights and latched the door behind her.

Saturday morning was clear and bright. But it was the middle of the morning before Ginny could escape from the house.

"Not an inch," her mother had said firmly. Ginny had given Mokey her morning feed and had finished her own breakfast. "You are not stirring one inch from this house, young lady, until you clean your room! Honestly, Ginny, how can you keep your stable so neat and your room so messy?"

Ginny didn't know, either. She flung her things into her drawers. She made her bed. Feeling a little guilty, she kicked an old notebook under the bed. Cleaning up her room was a chore. Taking care of Mokey was fun. It was as simple as that.

She snatched her hunt cap from the shelf. Then she tugged on her jacket and finally ran down to the stable.

She was supposed to meet Pam Jennings at her place in fifteen minutes. Ginny brushed Mokey quickly. She gave her a pat. She promised to do a better grooming job the next time. Then she bridled the pony and started on her way.

Mokey knew where they were going. She never minded being ridden alone. But she always liked going out with Pam's chestnut pony, Firefly.

Mokey broke into an eager trot and then into a strong canter. There were patches of silver frost on the shaded path through the woods. The air was crisp with the cold. Mokey gave a happy buck and a kick. She waved her long black tail.

Ginny pulled Mokey back to a quiet walk. They turned into the Jennings stable yard. She had expected to see Pam waiting on her pony. But the yard was empty. There were no hoof-prints in the smooth raked gravel in front of the wide white doors.

Ginny slipped off Mokey's back just as Pam started to roll back one of the doors.

"Hi!" she said to Ginny. Pam was out of breath. "I thought I heard you coming. Then Firefly started to whinny, so I knew it was you. Come on in."

Ginny led Mokey into the sunlit aisle between the two rows of box stalls. Firefly whinnied again from his stall. Mokey whinnied in answer.

"Gosh, they're noisy," said Pam. She put her hands over her ears. Once they had said hello, the ponies were quiet.

"I'm sorry, Ginny. I tried to call you in time," Pam said when she could be heard again. "But you'd already left. I can't ride Firefly today."

"What's the matter? Is he sick?" said Ginny with worry.

Pam glared at the closed door of the tack room.

"Michael's such a worrier," she said. "Firefly has a tiny cut on his fetlock. You can hardly see it. But Michael has that dumb pony wrapped up in enough bandages to keep a hospital going for a year."

She stopped and flushed with guilt. Michael was not in the tack room. He was just down the aisle with one of the other horses. He came limping out of the stall.

Michael was lean and strong. He had ridden steeplechasers in England. But then a bad fall had given him a limp and ended his racing career. He was still able to ride and care for horses. Mr. Jennings had bought two hunters from him in England a few years ago. He had then asked Michael to come with the horses to school them and care for the others in his stable. Michael had been with them ever since.

"Now, Miss Pam," he said crisply, "that cut's not much right now. But it will leave a scar if it's not cared for." Michael nodded to Ginny and went into the next stall.

"Glass," Pam said bitterly. "That pony is made of glass. Every time he gets the littlest lump or bump or bruise he ends up in slings."

"Never mind," Ginny said. "We'll have lots more days to ride together this winter. It's not like Mokey's going to be leaving, so it's not the same as it was last summer."

"That's true." Pam cheered up. "I guess I got used to feeling like each ride was going to be our last. Now that Mokey is really yours, it's different, isn't it?" She gave the pony a hug.

"I don't really want you to fall on your head again," she said to Ginny. "But it sure was fun to have Mokey here and take care of her when you couldn't ride those few weeks. You're not planning to break a leg or something this winter, are you? Just so I can have her here again?"

Ginny grinned.

"Not right away," she said. "It's much too nice having the new stable finished and Mokey home again. My father put the last of the shingles on the roof two days ago. It's all done just in time for the cold weather."

"Too bad." Pam ruffled Mokey's forelock cheerfully. "Ginny, if you've got a minute, come see what Michael's been working on this morning."

Ginny slipped a spare halter over Mokey's bridle. She cross-tied her in the aisle. Then she followed Pam into the warm tack room at the end of the stable.

# Chapter Two

A row of gleaming bridles hung high on one wall over a lower row of saddles. The bridles were protected by fitted linen dust covers. There were bright hunting prints on the other walls. Glass-doored cases displayed horse-show ribbons and silver trophies.

Ginny and Pam went into another room. Michael was inside whistling under his breath. He worked near a sinkful of steaming water. In the center of the cleaning room, a heavy hook hung from a chain on the ceiling. On the hook was the most confusing jumble of black leather that Ginny had ever seen.

"Isn't it beautiful?" said Pam. She was excited.

Ginny ran her finger over the glowing black leather. She was unsure.

"I'm sure it's wonderful," she said at last, "but what is it?"

"It's a harness!" said Pam. "Look, here's the bridle."

She lifted it off the hook. Ginny knew the blinkers were part of a driving bridle. She'd never seen one quite like this before. Not even in pictures. The blinkers were shining patent leather. On each of them was a delicate silver monogram. The brow band was also patent leather. Fastened over it was a chain pattern of square silver links.

"Mother used to show driving ponies," said Pam. She turned the bridle in her hands. The silver twinkled and glowed. "That was ages ago, of course, before she married my father. Then they started showing hunters instead. She kept this harness because it was one of her favorites. Michael keeps it in the storeroom. He gets it out to oil and clean it now and then. It's in great shape, isn't it? I wonder if anyone will ever use it again."

"If you take good care of nice leather, it lasts for years," said Michael. "But not if you leave it outside on a fence rail and let horses chew on it." He frowned at Pam. He took part of the harness off the hook. Then he went over to the sink.

"Oh, dear," whispered Pam. "He's still mad that I left Firefly's halter out in the paddock last week. I thought he'd forgotten about it by now." Pam sighed. "What do you want to do this morning, Ginny? Do you want to go on riding without me? It's too bad that dumb pony of mine had to hurt himself on a Saturday. We've waited through a whole week of school for a good long ride."

Ginny had been looking forward to spending the day with Mokey. But she didn't like to leave Pam with nothing to do. She hesitated.

Suddenly Pam spun around. The driving bridle was still in her hand.

"Michael!" she said with excitement. "Wouldn't this fit Mokey?"

Michael looked at the harness thoughtfully.

"Probably," he said. "The last pony your mother drove was her bay, Hackney. He was just about Mokey's size." He frowned through the steam. The soapy sponge was still in his hand. "Now, Miss Pam, don't you go getting any of your crazy ideas. You can't just throw a harness on a pony's back and drive it away. There's a lot more to it than that. It takes some time to break a pony to harness."

He turned back to the sink with a firm shake of his head. "And the pony cart can't be used. A friend of your father's borrowed it. The shaft was cracked when he brought it back."

"Darn." Pam slumped down on a stool. She put her chin in her hands.

Ginny felt a sharp stab of disappointment. She'd often wondered what it would be like to drive a pony. It looked like fun. She'd like to be able to drive a pony of her own.

Pam jumped to her feet. "Let's harness-break her anyway!" she said. "Michael, you'll show us how, won't you? You keep saying what wonderful manners Mokey has, and how smart she is. She'd be great in harness, wouldn't she? Then maybe we could get the shaft fixed."

"Miss Pam, there will be snow on the ground by the time you'll be able to use that cart. Then you couldn't take it out anyway," said Michael.

Pam grinned with pride. "Then I'll get the bells," she said. "Where are they, Michael?"

Even Michael had to smile at her excitement. "They're wrapped in a gray flannel bag. It's in the top drawer of the storage chest," he said.

Pam ran out of the room. Michael let the water out of the sink. He dried his hands. "I think I'm in for it this time," he said. "But Mokey is your pony, Miss Ginny. Do you want to teach her to drive?"

Ginny was confused. She didn't understand what Pam and her bells had to do with Mokey and the harness. But she nodded her head.

"It would be great," she said. "If Mrs. Jennings says it's okay for us to use her harness."

"It should be okay," said Michael. "It's good for tack to be used. But we'll ask her, of course, before we start." He shook his head in amusement. "Anything to keep you two girls from moaning around the stable, getting in my way."

But Ginny knew he didn't mean it. Michael seemed as happy with the idea as she was. Pam came racing back into the tack room. There was a shimmering, tinkling sound coming from something she was holding. It was hidden behind her back.

"Just look," she said to Ginny. "We've got a sleigh and these are the bells." She handed them to Ginny.

Ginny looked at the bells. She was speechless. There were three of them mounted on an arched metal stand. Every time Pam moved her hand, they chimed. They made a silvery, whispering sound.

"Have you ever seen anything so pretty in your entire life?" said Pam. "They fasten to the harness in the winter when you're driving a sleigh. I don't know how, but Michael does. Oh, Ginny, wouldn't it be fun to go sleighing this winter? It's something I've always wanted to do. But we never had a pony who was broken to harness to pull the sleigh before. At least, not since I can remember!"

"You won't have one this winter, if you don't get on with it." Michael took the bells from Ginny and put them on a shelf. "We won't need these for a while. The two of you can polish them up some rainy afternoon while you wait for it to snow. In the meantime, you both have a lot to do."

# Chapter Three

It seemed to take forever before Michael was finally happy with the way the harness fit Mokey. Ginny held Mokey in the stable aisle while Michael tested and fitted each strap and buckle. He moved slowly. He let Mokey get used to the feeling of each piece of harness before he added another.

Pam left the stable. She came back with news. Her mother was pleased that the harness was to be used, as long as it was done with Michael's supervision. She looked forward to being given a ride in the sleigh.

"If he ever gets done with all this before the snow thaws next spring," whispered Pam under her breath. Michael went to get a leather punch to shorten a strap.

Ginny patted Mokey. She smiled at Pam's impatience. Mokey moved her head. She was uncertain. The driving bridle felt strange to her.

Finally Michael was done.

"Right," he said. He was satisfied. "Lead her down the aisle and back again." He stepped back and nodded to Ginny. Ginny clucked to Mokey. The pony took a step or two forward. Then she suddenly skittered to one side. She bumped the wall. Then she bumped into Ginny and almost knocked her down.

"Ouch!" said Ginny. She hung on to Mokey's bridle. She was able to make the pony stand still. She rubbed her shoulder where the heavy driving bit had bruised it. Then she frowned at Mokey. "What was that all about?"

Mokey's eyes were rolling in a strange way. She was standing with her back humped up. "She's not used to the feeling of a harness," said Michael. "And it startled her when she moved. Pat her and talk to her. Now try again."

Mokey snorted her protest. She gave a halfhearted kick as she started to walk again. But soon she became familiar with the feeling of the harness on her back. She paid no more attention to it.

"Outside with her now," said Michael. He rolled back the wide white stable door. Ginny led Mokey around the stable yard. They stopped when Ginny was red in the face and out of breath and Mokey was bored.

"Very good," Michael said at last. Ginny took Mokey back inside the stable. Michael took the harness off. He put it back on again a few times. By this time Mokey paid no attention to any of the straps. They were dangling and tapping against her hindquarters and flanks. Sure that nothing was going to hurt her, she half closed her eyes. She relaxed one hip and stood dreamily in the sunny aisle. Michael showed Ginny how to put the harness on by herself.

"That should do it," Michael said at last. "We'll do the same tomorrow."

"You're kidding!" said Pam. "What about putting the reins on the bridle? What about—"

"That's enough for one day," Michael said firmly. "Slow and easy does it, Miss Pam. Hurry has no place with horses."

"Let's go look at the sleigh," said Pam. The harness had been returned to the tack room. Michael had shooed the girls out of his way. "It's in the storage barn beyond the paddocks. It's been there for years. I don't know when it was last used."

The two girls both got on Mokey. They trotted down the lane that ran between the white-fenced paddocks. Ginny held Mokey. Pam tugged at the doors of the barn. They finally opened with a shriek. Inside, dim gray light filled the old hay barn. A small red sleigh with delicate, curled runners stood in a corner.

"It needs a new paint job. But Michael said he came down here and checked it just a little while ago. It's in good enough shape to be used," said Pam. At first Mokey didn't want to walk into the barn with its wooden floor. It made a funny noise under her hooves. After a little bit of coaxing, Ginny was able to lead her over to the sleigh.

"Gosh, it's pretty," said Ginny. There was awe in her voice. She ran her hand over the curve of the shaft. "It looks just like a Christmas card."

Mokey blew softly down the back of Ginny's neck. The two girls and the pony stood admiring the little sleigh in silence.

"Well," said Pam finally, "it's going to be great. But I'm really glad you started breaking Mokey today. Otherwise, with the way Michael does things, it would have been the middle of next summer before Michael said she was ready!"

\* \* \*

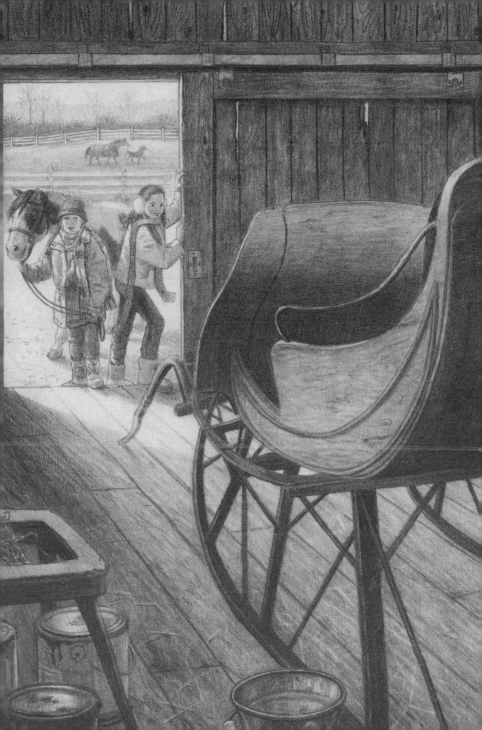

The next day, and every chance she had after school and on weekends, Ginny worked with Mokey. She was a little puzzled but willing. Michael watched over them. The long driving reins were run through the rings on the harness and buckled to the bit. Ginny learned how to hold them. She also learned how to manage the light driving whip at the same time.

At first it was hard for Mokey to understand why Ginny was walking so far behind her. She was used to Ginny being up on her back. The pony walked ahead of Ginny as though she were lost. But as the days went by, both Ginny and Mokey began to feel more sure of themselves.

Ginny groaned one evening after dinner as she got to her feet. "You wouldn't believe how stiff I am!" she said. "I've walked miles today!"

"I thought you were teaching that Moke of yours to drive," said her father. "Why all the walking? No wheels?"

"No wheels," said Ginny. "Just me on my

26

legs and Mokey on hers. Even if we had any wheels, which we don't, we still wouldn't be using them. Michael says Mokey and I don't know enough."

At the next practice session, Michael fastened the traces of the harness to a log. It had a sturdy ring bolted onto each end.

"Watch your pony," he said to Ginny. He stepped back out of the way. "She may not like the sound of the log dragging behind her."

Ginny nodded and clucked to Mokey. Mokey took a step and then stopped. She was puzzled by the feeling of the traces getting tighter. Ginny clucked gently again. She touched the pony lightly with the whip. Michael came to lead the pony forward. The log moved with a grating sound over the ground.

Mokey raised her head. She clamped her tail between her legs. But Michael and Ginny both calmed her. Ginny's hands were gentle and steady on the reins. The brief moment of worry was soon over.

"I don't know who has the most patience," said Pam to Ginny. "You or Michael or Mokey." She jumped down from the stable-yard wall where she'd been watching. "I'd be bored to death by now."

Ginny just smiled without speaking. It took a lot of focus, but the pony was walking steadily now. She paid no attention at all to the bumping drag of the log behind her. With a tiny flourish of the tip of her whip, Ginny drove Mokey out through the gates and down the lane between the paddocks.

Relaxed and obedient, Mokey walked and jogged ahead of Ginny. She stopped and started smoothly whenever she was asked. She made circles and turns evenly and without hesitation.

Everything had gone well.

By the end of that afternoon, Ginny rode Mokey home through the gathering dusk. She knew that both she and Mokey were ready.

# Chapter Four

Michael thought so, too. The sleigh was brought up from the barn. Michael replaced a loop of cracked leather. He rubbed leather polish into another loop. He oiled the bolts that fastened the shafts to the sleigh. Ginny and Pam dusted and polished the old, chipped paint as well as they could. Then they helped to push the sleigh into a small shed near the stable. They waited anxiously for snow.

Ginny had to be content with riding Mokey alone. The cut on Firefly's leg had healed perfectly. But he celebrated by bucking Pam off the first day he was ridden. Racing back to the stable, he slipped and fell as he turned through the gates. Then he slid on the rough gravel. Now he was back in bandages again.

The weather grew colder. Ice formed in lacy patterns at the edges of the streams. The blacksmith welded rough metal on Mokey's shoes the next time she was shod.

"Just a touch of borium on the toes and heels to keep her from slipping on the ice or packed snow," the blacksmith told Ginny. "Got to keep at least one of these ponies on its feet!" He went to pull the shoes off Firefly. He didn't need to wear them while he was being kept in his stall.

But still there was no snow. Ginny took Mokey out in harness at least once a week to keep in practice. But even she and Mokey were starting to get bored. It wasn't as much fun anymore.

Thanksgiving came. Then the short vacation was over. Ginny and Pam listened eagerly to the weather reports. They looked hopefully at the sky every morning before they went to school. The ice skating was the best there had been in years. The ponds froze smoothly in deep, black ice without snow on the surface.

The ground froze until it was as hard as concrete. Ginny's rides became slow and dull. The footing was too hard and rough to do much more than walk or jog slowly. Mokey grew fatter and shaggier every day. But still there was no snow.

"Let's move to Canada! Or the Alps or the North Pole!" Ginny said with anger the next Saturday morning. The sun rose in a cold but cloudless sky. "There's got to be snow for the sleigh somewhere in the world!"

She stomped bitterly down the hill to feed Mokey. The pony was whinnying loudly for her breakfast. Ginny had forgotten to put her gloves on. Her hands hurt when she pulled back the metal bolts and swung open the doors that led from the stall to the paddock. Mokey came charging out with her tail in the air. She was whistling through her nostrils. She greeted the cold morning with a buck and a kick of delight. Ginny shook her head gloomily. Her cold hands were shoved into her pockets. She watched her pony prance cheerfully across the paddock.

It was all very well for Mokey to be so bright and gay. But the stall needed a good cleaning. Ginny had skimped a little through the week because there had been exams almost every day. The wheels were probably frozen on the manure cart. A new bag of grain had split open and spilled. The hoofpick was lost. Ginny sighed and went to get Mokey's grain. Firefly was still lame and Pam had gone skiing. It was going to be a long, dull weekend.

The alarm clock buzzed. Ginny flung one hand out from under the warmth of the blankets. She slapped at the clock. It fell over and became silent.

Ginny groaned. She opened her eyes.

Monday morning. Yuck. She pulled the blankets up over her head. She tried to remember whether or not she'd corrected her math paper over the weekend.

Even through the muffling blankets she could hear the clink of dishes and the sound of running water in the kitchen. She'd better get up and feed Mokey if she wanted to get it done before breakfast.

She stumbled sleepily out of bed. She walked across the room. She was shivering. With a giant yawn, Ginny started to get dressed.

Her arms and back were stiff. Ginny tried clearing her throat. There were a lot of colds and things going around school at this time of year. Maybe she was coming down with something. Maybe she was getting sick and wouldn't have to go to school today, after all.

She coughed hopefully and then sighed. She knew very well she was stiff because she'd ridden for long hours the day before. She also knew she had not done her math. Gloomily, she tugged a sweater over her head.

Her mother tapped lightly on the door and opened it.

"You might as well go back to bed," she said. "No school today!"

"No school?" Ginny's head shot through the tight neck of her sweater. She stared at her mother.

"Just look out the window." Ginny's mother smiled. Suddenly wide awake, Ginny flew over to the window and pushed back the curtains.

It must have snowed all night. It was still snowing hard. Drifts rolled across the lawn. They buried the small bushes in the garden and rippled across the driveway.

"Beautiful," Ginny said out loud. "Beautiful!"

She snatched up a sock and stood hopping on one foot. She looked out at the snow. From the kitchen she could hear the low sound of the local radio station report: "All schools in the area are closed for the day due to the heavy storm."

"Hear you have a snow day today!" her father greeted her as Ginny came into the warm kitchen. "Why don't you go back to bed?"

"Bed!" Ginny said in horror. "But it's snowing!"

Her father smiled. He'd only been teasing. The radio was now giving the weather report: "Up to six inches of snow is expected to fall before stopping at noon. The sky should clear during the afternoon, with slowly rising temperatures."

"Perfect," said Ginny with a shiver of excitement. She drank a glass of orange juice. Then she pulled on her snow boots and jacket. She ran outdoors into the snow.

All the world smelled cold and clean. The snow swirled everywhere. It covered the tree branches. It filled the air with dancing patterns. With the flakes melting on her face,

Ginny ran down to the stable to give Mokey her breakfast. Pam was on the phone when Ginny got back to the house. She was wild with excitement. Ginny promised she'd be over just as soon as she could.

"But I have to wait an hour after Mokey's had her grain. I just fed her," Ginny said. "Do you think Michael will remember to put the bells on the harness?"

"I'll remind him," said Pam, "just in case. See you soon!"

Ginny was as impatient as Pam. The hour passed slowly. She had a quick breakfast. She brushed and rebraided her hair. Then she shoveled snow away from the garage door with her father. He drove away with the tire chains jangling on the rear wheels of the car.

At last it was time to get Mokey. The eager pony danced through the snowy woods. She followed the slight tracing of the familiar path through the trees. The woods were full of mys-

tery and a gentle, hushed silence. There was
no sound of hoofbeats. There was nothing but
the whispering of the snow sifting through the
trees and Mokey's soft breathing.

The snowflakes fell like powdered sugar
on Mokey's black forelock and over the hood

of Ginny's jacket. The snow swirled around them in the close silence of the woods. Ginny thought dreamily that this must be what it would be like to be a tiny figure inside a snow globe.

She was almost sorry when the ride was over. But her heart jumped with excitement as Pam slid the stable door back to welcome Ginny and her snowy pony inside.

No one said very much. Pam was sparkling with hidden excitement. Ginny focused on fitting the harness in place. And Michael had not forgotten the bells. They rang lightly as Ginny finished. Mokey started to paw the ground eagerly.

Ginny hesitated. "Are you sure it's all right for the harness to get all wet in the snow?" she finally asked Michael. He had been watching without comment. "Maybe we should wait until it stops."

"Silly," said Pam with a giggle before Michael could answer. "In the olden days, do you think people stayed home if it snowed? Horses and carriages went out in all kinds of weather!"

"The pony's going to be all right," Michael said briefly. Ginny felt a little better. Michael understood. Now that the moment had finally come, Ginny was nervous. Mokey suddenly looked big and strange in the black and silver harness. The snowy fields and lanes outside no longer looked soft and inviting. They looked scary and full of hidden dangers. Maybe they hadn't practiced enough. Maybe the bells would scare the pony.

Ginny knew if she waited one more moment, she'd never be able to take the important step of actually fastening Mokey's traces to the sleigh. She barely gave herself time to put on her gloves. Then she nodded quickly to Pam and led Mokey outside.

Pam had pulled the sleigh from the shed. It was waiting in the stable yard. Pam held the pony. Ginny helped Michael ease the curved red shafts through the loops of the harness. Ginny was shivering so hard that her teeth chattered. She tried to follow Michael's quick hands. He fastened the traces and buckled the harness to the sleigh. But she was much too nervous. There were too many things to remember.

"I'll teach you to do this another time," said Michael. "But this is the first time out. We don't want to keep the pony standing any longer than we must."

He stood up. He checked one last buckle. Then he stepped back. He and Ginny looked at the waiting pony and the pretty red sleigh in a moment of silence.

"Oh, come on!" said Pam. Mokey tossed her head and made the silver bells ring. "Aren't you ready yet?"

# Chapter Five

Ginny's throat was so dry she could hardly swallow.

"In you go," Michael said to her. "Gently, now." He went to Mokey's head and held her. Ginny stepped quietly into the sleigh. She took the reins and the whip in her hands.

It felt very strange to be sitting so high and so far away from Mokey. Ginny gulped again. Michael spoke softly to Mokey. He turned to see if Ginny was ready. Ginny nodded stiffly. Pam stepped back. Michael clucked to the pony.

Mokey took one step. The traces got tighter from the weight of the standing sleigh.

Mokey stopped. She was unsure.

"Come on, Mokey!" Ginny said. Her voice was hoarse. Michael patted the pony and clucked again. The pony lowered her head and moved forward.

Once it was started, the sleigh slipped silently and easily through the snow. The bells on the harness chimed softly. They were safely through the stable-yard gates. Michael stepped away from Mokey's head. The reins came alive in Ginny's hands. She felt Mokey's mouth with the reins through the bit. The pony responded. She turned down the lane leading between the paddocks.

Mokey was walking more freely now and with more sureness.

"Miss Pam," Michael said quietly, "you walk by the pony's shoulder for a bit. If there's any trouble, be ready to take hold of her head. Otherwise, leave her alone."

In one quick and silent movement, he was in the sleigh beside Ginny. Ginny handed the reins to Michael. The snow fell and stung her face. The harness bells rang softly. But Ginny didn't notice. She was too busy watching Michael's hands on the reins and listening to what he said.

They drove at a quiet walk down the lane. They made a wide sweep around the old storage barn. Then they started back toward the stable. They passed the gates. They went around the wide sweep of driveway in front of the Jennings house. Once they passed the stable yard again, Michael let Mokey move on into a jogging trot.

By now Pam was completely out of breath. At Michael's nod, she flung herself down on a snowbank. She waved as the sleigh went on. Mokey was moving evenly. She was more sure of herself. Michael nodded. He was pleased.

"Good," he said. Ginny glowed.

Michael drew Mokey back to a walk.

"Here you go," he said to Ginny. He handed her the reins.

Mokey felt different hands on the reins. She threw her head up and stopped. Michael got out of the sleigh. He was at the pony's head before Ginny even saw him start to move.

"Gently, little lady," he said to the pony. He led Mokey for a few minutes. Then he swung silently back into the sleigh.

Ginny's hands grew stiff with cold and tension. Her head spun. She tried to remember everything Michael had taught her. The tracks of the sleigh runners had run so straight

when Michael drove. Now they snaked and wobbled behind them as she drove her pony down the lane. Mokey felt the nervousness in Ginny's hands. She kept stopping. Once she tried to back up. But Michael was always quick to move to her head to get the pony moving forward again.

Slowly the marks of the sleigh runners in the snow started to straighten out. Michael was in the sleigh now more than he was out of it. Once or twice, he even nodded his

approval as Ginny made a wide turn. The pony moved evenly between the shafts.

The moment finally came when Michael stepped out of the sleigh and waved to Pam. Her dark eyes were shining with excitement. Pam slipped silently onto the red leather seat beside Ginny.

Mokey broke into an easy jog. The silver bells rang. Ginny heard the gentle sound of the bells and the hushed hiss of the runners through the snow. The reins began to feel comfortable in her hands. Strong and cheerful, Mokey trotted along the drifted lane. Her breath made twin puffs of steam in the cold air.

They started to sweep past the stable yard again. Michael shook his head and raised his hand. Ginny was reluctant, but she drew Mokey back to a walk and then to a stop. Michael went to the pony's head. He gave her a lump of sugar.

"Very good, Miss Ginny. Very nice indeed. But your pony's had enough for one day."

Ginny felt guilty. She saw the clouds of steam rising from Mokey's sweating sides. She noticed how heavily the pony was breathing. She jumped quickly out of the sleigh. Then she helped to lead Mokey into the stable yard. Pam ran to get a cooler. She threw it over Mokey's back. Together the girls covered the hot pony with the wide blanket. It would keep her from getting chilled. Michael unharnessed her from the sleigh.

Ginny felt tired when she had gotten out of the sleigh. Then Mokey had been unharnessed. She was taken into the stable to be rubbed and walked and then rubbed again. After that, Ginny felt as though she could never take another step again.

Pam helped by taking over Mokey's cooling out. Then they carried the heavy harness into the tack room. Every salty sweat mark had to be saddle-soaped clean under Michael's watchful eye. Even the bit and all the buckles had to be dried. They were polished back to their original shine. Then Michael finally let her hang the harness in its place in the tack room.

Ginny fell onto a hay bale in the stable aisle. She sighed wearily. Michael ran his hand over Mokey's chest. He shook his head in disapproval.

"The pony is still warm," he said.

"But, Michael!" Pam said with a wail. "Her coat's so long! It's never going to dry out!"

"This is always a problem with an unclipped pony," said Michael. "And that's why she tired so quickly. I'd be happy to clip her for you, Miss Ginny. But you won't be able to turn her out in the paddock for very long during the day. She won't have her winter coat to protect her. While you're in school, you can't be there to let her in or out of her stall as the weather changes."

They all looked at the shaggy pony in silence.

"But you could get a New Zealand rug," said Michael. "It's a special blanket made of canvas and lined with wool. It's windproof and waterproof. It's made to be worn as a turn-out blanket. A plain stable blanket isn't strong enough for this."

Ginny made a face. She had already learned this. She had let Mokey out into the paddock wearing her blanket one cold morning. By noon one of the webbing surcingles was torn. One of the two leather chest straps was broken. It had taken a week to have it fixed. She knew better than to do it again. The blanket came off before the pony went out.

"I bet they're expensive," said Ginny.

Michael nodded. "But they do last for many, many years."

Ginny frowned at Mokey. "I hope you're worth all this," she said. "I've been saving my allowance for a long time for a stereo. But I think I'd much rather have a New Zealand rug for Moke." She got stiffly to her feet. "We've been trying to get her cooled out and dry for almost two hours. I just can't bear the thought of ever having to go through this again. No matter how much fun it is to drive her in the sleigh!"

"I'll take her for a while," said Michael. "She's almost done."

Ginny was grateful. She followed Pam up to the house. The two girls curled up in front of an open fire in the study. They sipped steaming mugs of cocoa.

"You know what?" said Ginny. She squinted her eyes and watched the steam curl up out of her mug. "It all looks so simple in the Christmas cards, doesn't it? Jingle bells, put the pony to the sleigh and away we go. Nothing about harness-breaking the beasts. Or learning how to drive them. Or cooling them out and cleaning all that harness afterwards. Do you realize the hours we spent working for that one morning of sleighing?"

She shook her head in wonder. "Not that it wasn't worth it. It was wonderful. I can't wait to go out again. But it does make you stop and think a little." There was an old English coaching scene in a heavy gold frame over the fireplace. Ginny looked at it briefly and shuddered. "Four horses, can you imagine? All that muddy harness—"

"And four hot, dirty horses to cool out and groom and put away," Pam broke in with a smile. "Here, you'd better have another cookie. You still need enough energy left to ride Mokey home."

# Chapter Six

The New Zealand rug was ordered from the
tack shop. After it had been delivered, Michael
clipped Mokey.

Without her shaggy winter coat, the pony
looked very strange and bare to Ginny. And
Mokey's back was more slippery. Ginny found
it was harder to stay on when she rode the
pony home again in the late afternoon. Mokey
wasn't behaving very well. That didn't help.
Every time Ginny asked her to trot, the pony
humped her back and skittered sideways. The
first try at a canter sent Mokey off into a series
of bucks and kicks. They almost put Ginny off.

Mad and out of breath, Ginny quickly pulled Mokey back to a walk. The pony acted like something was bothering her, like a twisted girth. This didn't make much sense. Ginny was riding bareback, as she always did.

Ginny got home and turned Mokey out into her paddock. Then she understood what had been causing the problem. Mokey trotted unevenly across the paddock to her stall. Ginny could see that snow was kicking up from the pony's hooves. It was tickling her on her newly clipped stomach. Ginny laughed out loud at the pony's upset look. She knew that Mokey would soon get used to it.

Wednesday was a half day at school. Pam had a piano lesson to make up. She couldn't ride. Michael gave Ginny the message when she rode Mokey over to the Jennings stable. He then offered to spend the afternoon teaching Ginny how to harness her pony to the sleigh.

It was warm and sunny in the sheltered stable yard. Mokey stood waiting. She was half asleep in the sun. Ginny played with the straps of the harness. Within a short time, they all made sense to her. She could harness and un-harness the pony. Michael didn't find a single mistake.

Ginny finished up by driving the sleigh alone. She felt more and more sure of herself and of her pony. But the snow was getting soggy in the sun. The sleigh would no longer slide easily.

"But we're in great shape now," Ginny told Michael. She finished cleaning the harness. Then she went into the tack room to put it away. "Mokey's clipped. I know how to har-ness her to the sleigh by myself. All we need now is more fresh snow."

Ginny got her wish. Christmas vacation started with a two-day storm. The flurry and the excitement of the holidays slipped by quickly. It snowed again on New Year's Eve. Ginny rode Mokey over to Pam's the next morning. The sky was still dark with the look of more snow to come.

Ginny found Pam stomping up and down the aisle of the stable. They had planned to go riding in the fresh snow that morning. But Firefly had gotten a cough during the night. Michael had told her that the pony could not be ridden. Then he had gone off to visit a friend.

"Do you want to go out in the sleigh again, since you can't ride Firefly today?" Ginny asked.

Pam frowned. She kicked at a snowbank in the yard. "I guess so," she said finally. "But it's pretty boring now, isn't it? I mean, just going back and forth in the lane and in the driveway. We've done that lots of times. I don't see why we can't take the sleigh out on the roads."

"Usually they're plowed and salted," Ginny told her. "And the snow melts too fast.

Especially when the sun comes out. Then there's not enough snow left for the sleigh."

"But there is today," said Pam eagerly, "and it's going to snow again. Come on, let's do it. Think how much fun it would be."

Ginny hesitated. "I don't think Michael would let us," she said at last.

"Oh, who cares?" said Pam. "He's such a wet blanket. You know that. Don't do this, Miss Pam. Don't do that. Don't ride your poor pony today. He's got a little cough. Worry, worry, worry. That's all he does." She shook her short, curly hair impatiently. "Come on, Ginny, I'm so bored! There's nothing else to do. We don't have to go very far if you don't want to."

Ginny straightened Mokey's black forelock and smoothed it over the brow band.

"Okay," she said at last. After all, it was Pam's sleigh, not her own. It seemed the least she could do, if Pam wanted it so badly. And Ginny had to admit that it was getting a little boring just driving around the Jennings place.

Ginny pressed Mokey's bridle reins into Pam's hand. "I'll go and get the harness," she said.

The runners of the red sleigh slipped easily over the packed snow on the road. Mokey reached lightly for the bit. She waved her long black tail. Then she made her stride longer. The silver bells on the harness made a brighter sound than they ever had before.

The snow-laden branches of the trees arched over them. They spun along the narrow, winding road. There was no sound anywhere but the musical chiming of the bells and the hushed whisper of the runners on the snow. It began to snow again, softly. Time stood still. They had gone several miles. Suddenly Ginny saw how far they were from home.

"We'd better find a place to turn around pretty soon," she said. She brushed the snowflakes from her face. She pulled Mokey

down to a walk. "The road's too narrow here to turn a sleigh. That was great, wasn't it?" She grinned at Pam. "This was a wonderful idea."

The road forked at the bottom of the hill. Ginny swept the sleigh around in a wide circle. She looked back with pride at the even marks the runners left in the snow. Mokey broke into a happy jog. This set the bells jingling softly. It was like they were singing to themselves.

Pam sighed happily. "I heard somebody say once that whatever you do on New Year's Day you'll do all year long," she said. "I sure hope the rest of the year is as much fun as this."

Ginny didn't answer. Her hands gripped the reins. Something was wrong. Mokey had raised her head. Her back grew stiff. Her ears were pricked forward in alarm.

"Hang on," Ginny said to Pam in a tight voice. "I don't know what it is. But something is scaring Mokey."

The two girls knew in a moment. They

heard what Mokey had heard a few seconds before. It was the low, muffled roar of a snowplow. It was coming toward them.

Pam's face went white. She grabbed Ginny's arm. "What are we going to do? We're going to be killed!"

"Let go of me!" Ginny said sharply. "I can't drive with you hanging on to my arm!" She shortened the reins. Mokey had broken stride. She dropped back to an unsure walk.

The snowplow was on the road somewhere ahead of them. It was hidden by a bend in the road. Mokey had broken out in a nervous sweat. Her head was moving from side to side. She kept trying to stop. Ginny knew that the scared pony was getting herself ready to turn around. She wanted to run away from the terrible roar. It was coming closer all the time. But with all the storms they'd been having, the banks were piled high on both sides of the road with plowed snow. There was just not enough room to turn the sleigh around.

# Chapter Seven

The glowing headlights and flashing red warning lights of the plow came into view. They were at the far end of the road. Mokey reared in fright. Above the loud clashing sound of the harness bells, Ginny could hear Mokey's hind shoes slipping. They cut through the snowy surface, down to the icy road underneath. For one scary moment, Ginny thought Mokey was losing her balance. She thought she was going to fall backward onto the sleigh.

"Hang on!" Ginny cried to Pam. Mokey got her balance. She started to rear again. The bells jangled harshly. The thin driving whip whistled through the air, just once. Startled and surprised, Mokey pushed forward.

The sleigh jolted and rocked. Ginny was shouting. Mokey was galloping straight toward the terrifying plow.

They could see the white plumes of snow curling away from the wide blade of the plow. The flashing lights grew brighter through the falling flakes. Mokey was weaving crazily back and forth across the road. But Ginny was doing the only thing she could think of to do. She remembered having seen a driveway. It was not far ahead, just past a snow-heaped clump of rhododendron bushes. If she could keep Mokey going, they could reach the driveway in time to get out of the way of the plow.

Mokey skidded to a sudden stop. She tried to rear again. Pam screamed. Ginny shouted. The pony pushed forward again. There was a low bank of snow across the opening to the drive. But there was no time to slow down. Ginny steadied her pony as well as she could. Then she swung her into the drive.

There was silence. There was cold and darkness everywhere. Ginny lay very still. She couldn't open her eyes. Everything was black. She was afraid to try to move.

She heard the gentle chiming of bells. At least she knew that Mokey wasn't lying dead in the snow with a broken neck. Dead ponies didn't ring sleigh bells. Having decided this, Ginny felt better. She tried to sit up.

No wonder everything was cold and dark. She'd landed facedown in a snowdrift. Ginny blinked. She brushed the snow from her face. She looked around quickly. She had to know what awful damage had been done.

Pam was sitting in the snow next to Ginny. Her head was in her hands. Her shoulders were shaking under her red jacket.

Ginny jumped to her feet in alarm. "What's the matter? Where are you hurt?" she asked in a shaking voice. Muffled gasps and choking sounds came from Pam. She looked up at Ginny with tears in her eyes.

"I never saw anything so funny in my life!" she said. Ginny realized with anger that Pam was laughing.

Ginny spun around to see what was so funny. She didn't know that she was covered from head to foot with snow. She looked like a walking snowman.

Mokey was standing peacefully in the drifted driveway. Clouds of steam were rising from her sweaty sides. The red sleigh was half tipped over behind her. It was at a strange angle. The reins were curling in dark tangles all around her legs. She was pawing lightly at the snow to see if there was any grass to eat underneath.

"I'm sorry, Ginny. I didn't mean to scare you." Pam giggled helplessly. "But you really looked so funny with your feet sticking up out of the snow. And wouldn't you know Mokey would try to find something to eat at a time like this?"

Still half angry, Ginny walked stiffly over to Mokey. The pony turned her head. She reached over to Ginny's pocket, begging for a lump of sugar.

Ginny dug in her pocket. She found the damp lump of sugar. Mokey had known it was there. She gave it to Mokey absently. Then Ginny looked the pony over. She checked the harness and the sleigh.

Ginny took off one glove. She ran her hand over Mokey's legs. She felt for cuts or bruises. She couldn't find any. Pam looked sorry but was still giggling a little. She came to hold the pony. Ginny finished checking the sleigh. It took only a light push to set it back on its runners.

"Lead Mokey forward a few steps to see if she's all right," Ginny told Pam. Mokey moved through the snow without any trouble. Ginny shrugged her shoulders.

"Nothing seems to be wrong," she said, almost crossly. She found she was yelling to be heard. The snowplow was going by the opening to the drive where they stood. The flashing lights made orange and red flickering patterns on the snow. Then it was gone. It left a high mound of white where the opening to the drive had been.

"Oh, great!" Ginny said. She sounded mad. "Now what are we going to do? We're going to be stuck in here until spring!"

"The driver couldn't have known we were in here," Pam said. She pointed toward the plow. It roared as it was moving away. "I'm sure he never even saw us."

Ginny rubbed Mokey gently between her ears.

"I'm sorry," she said both to Mokey and to Pam. "I didn't mean to sound so mad. I was so scared. I just couldn't believe everything was all right." Pam smiled. She understood. Ginny gave Mokey another lump of melting sugar. She squinted through the falling snow, taking in their problem.

There was no question about it. They really did have a problem. Mokey and the sleigh were facing away from the road. The driveway where they stood had been plowed earlier in the winter, but not recently. The snow was knee-deep all the way to the house. The house was set so far from the road that they could barely see it.

"It looks as though there's just flat lawn next to the driveway," said Pam. "We can't ruin it with Mokey's hooves at this time of year. The ground is too frozen. That house sits down in that little hollow. The snow may have drifted pretty deep. Maybe we should try to turn around right here."

Ginny looked at the level snow. She was doubtful.

Anything could be hidden under the

snow. A low wire fence. Or an old toy wagon. Or even a narrow, icy stream with sharp, rocky banks.

She shivered. "We can't stay here forever. Mokey's getting cold. We'll just have to try it and be very careful, I guess."

Pam walked ahead to feel for hidden obstacles under the snow. Ginny followed. She led Mokey. They made a wide circle. Then they proudly stopped where they'd started. But this time they were facing toward the road.

"Now all we have to do is get from here to there," said Ginny. She felt more cheerful. Then she had another long look at the high wall of fresh snow. It was between the pony and the road.

Pam climbed up over the drift and then came back.

"It's soft," she told Ginny. "At least it's not icy, but it's pretty deep. Do you think Mokey and the sleigh can get through?"

It was Ginny's turn to laugh. "I don't think

we have much choice," she said. "We're going to have to try." She climbed into the sleigh. She took a deep breath. "You lead Mokey to get her started," she said to Pam. "But be ready to jump out of the way if the sleigh tips over."

"Okay." Pam patted Mokey. She clucked to the pony. Then she started toward the drift.

Mokey pushed ahead. Pam cheered her on. The pony stopped when the snow suddenly started to get deeper. But she quickly pushed forward again.

Mokey struggled through the deep drift. The sleigh rose up behind her. It looked like it was being lifted on the crest of a wave. The delicate sleigh rocked and swayed as it reached the top. For one awful moment, Ginny was sure it was going to tip over. But Pam steadied Mokey with her voice and her hands. The pony braced herself. The sleigh dipped forward. It slid gently and evenly down onto the freshly plowed road.

"Wow" was all Ginny could say.

Pam grinned. She got into the sleigh beside Ginny.

"That must be what it's like to launch a lifeboat in a storm," she said.

Mokey turned her head to look back at the two girls.

"I think," said Ginny, "she wants to go home."

"Great idea," said Pam. Ginny pulled in the reins and clucked to her pony. Mokey set out at an even, smooth trot. The bells began their soft chime.

It was cold enough so that the plow had left a thin layer of snow on the road. The runners bit through to the road surface with a grating sound. It made the two girls and the pony give a startled jump each time.

It was with a huge sigh of relief that Ginny steadied Mokey back to a quiet walk. She turned her into the Jennings drive.

"Not a word of this to Michael," warned Pam.

Ginny giggled. "Do you think I'm out of my mind?" she said. "Anyway, he doesn't have to know we've even been off your place! We could have just been puttering around here as we always have before. Unless we tell him, how could he ever know?"

Mokey was hot and tired. Ginny felt guilty. She let her walk slowly. She hoped the pony would look cool enough and rested by the time they reached the stable.

"Yuck," said Ginny under her breath. They started down the lane that led to the stable.

"What's the matter?" asked Pam.

"Just look who's there," said Ginny. She nodded toward the stable-yard gates.

"Uh-oh," said Pam. "And I can tell, even from here, he's really mad."

Michael stood waiting. His hands were on his hips. He looked very stern and grim. He nodded coldly, just once. Ginny drew Mokey to a smooth stop at the gates. Ginny hoped he might comment on how nicely she'd stopped.

In fact, she wished that he'd say just about anything at all. She just wanted him to break the chilling silence.

But Michael just nodded shortly once more. He stood looking at the tired pony and the uneasy girls in the sleigh. Then he turned and went into the stable without a word.

Pam sighed. "I have never," she said slowly, "gotten away with one single thing without Michael knowing all about it. Not in all the years he's been here."

In silence they unharnessed the pony. They threw a cooler over her back. Then they took her inside the stable. They put the sleigh away and carried the harness to the tack room. The harness was covered in sweat. They hung it on the cleaning hook. Then they started working on it with hot, soapy sponges.

There was no sign of Michael. Ginny scrubbed at the bit. She looked over her shoulder from time to time.

"Whew." Pam stopped working for a moment. She pushed the hair back out of her eyes. "There's a mile of this thing, isn't there!" Ginny nodded silently. She looped the straps and tucked them into place as they were cleaned. At last the whole harness was done. They hung it back in its place.

Pam folded the cooler. Ginny bridled Mokey and swung up onto her back. Pam looked around quickly. She opened the door to let Mokey and Ginny walk outside. Then she whispered, "I don't care how mad Michael is. It was fun, anyway!"

Ginny waved good-bye. She was grateful to escape without seeing Michael again. Mokey was very tired. As soon as they reached the path through the woods, Ginny got off. She pulled the reins over the pony's head and led her toward home. It was getting colder and starting to snow heavily again. Ginny made a face at the low clouds. She decided that even she and Mokey had had enough snow for a while.

# Chapter Eight

"You look worried," Ginny's mother said.

"I am," said Ginny. She was in the kitchen stirring bran and oats and hot water together. She was making a hot mash for Mokey. She added a little salt. Then she put a folded towel over the top of the bucket to let the mash steam. "Gosh, that stuff has a wonderful smell," she said. "No wonder ponies love it."

She started to cut up a carrot to add to the mash. "I'm worried about Mokey," she said to her mother. "I can't understand what's wrong with her. She's fit. I feed her well. But her ribs are starting to show a little bit even though her blanket hardly goes around her middle."

"What does Michael say?" asked Mrs. Anderson.

"He just told me she was getting too fat and that I was probably giving her too much hay. But he told me that when he first clipped her. That was before Christmas. So I gave her less hay. Now she looks kind of strange. He went back to England to visit his family for a few weeks. He hasn't seen her for a while.

"Thank goodness," she added under her breath. Nothing had ever been said about the sleigh ride on the road on New Year's Day. Maybe he would have forgotten all about it by the time he got back.

"Do you think it might be a good idea to ask the vet to have a look at her?" asked her mother. "Ginny, for goodness' sakes, don't give Mokey all the carrots. We need some for the salad tonight!"

"I'm sorry." Ginny grinned at her mother.

She quickly put the cut-up carrots into the mash. "I'll go call Dr. Nichols and ask him to come see Mokey."

Dr. Nichols came the next afternoon. He left an hour later with a smile and a cheerful wave.

Ginny stomped into the living room. She forgot to take off her boots. They were covered in snow. She stood in front of the fire. She felt numb.

"You'll never guess what," she said with a croak to her mother and father. Her father put down his newspaper. Her mother looked up from her book.

"Mokey's in foal," said Ginny.

"In foal?" said her mother.

"You mean she's pregnant?" asked her father. Ginny nodded. She was speechless.

Mr. Anderson folded his newspaper. He began to laugh. Ginny frowned at her father.

"It isn't funny!" she said. Then she began

to smile. "I guess it is," she said. "Imagine her being in foal all this time, without our knowing anything about it!"

"When is she due to have it?" asked Mrs. Anderson.

"Dr. Nichols says it's hard to tell with horses and ponies. Especially with a first foal. But he thinks around the end of March or the beginning of April. She was probably bred just before she came here. It takes eleven months until the foal is born." Ginny shook her head in wonder. "I can't really believe it yet. I keep thinking I'm dreaming."

She looked down at the snow from her boots. It was melting on the living room rug. "Help!" she said breathlessly. "I'd better get out of here. And I've got to call Pam!"

Pam was wild with excitement and envy. "I've always wanted to raise a foal!" she said.

"You can share Mokey's," said Ginny.

There was a short silence. Both girls tried to picture Mokey with a foal. Ginny found it impossible.

"I can't wait to tell Michael," Pam said with a giggle. "Mokey sure fooled him! I bet this will be the biggest surprise of his life!"

But Michael took the news quite calmly when he came back from his vacation. It was a chilly, cloudy afternoon. Ginny rode over to the Jennings place on Mokey. It had started to rain. Then the rain turned to sleet. Ginny put Mokey into the extra stall. Then she went into the tack room with Pam to welcome Michael home and to tell him the news.

Michael nodded as Ginny told him. "But she did fool you, didn't she, Michael?" said Pam.

Michael smiled at her. "Miss Pam, a lot of horsemen have been taken by surprise by a lot of mares for a lot of years. When I was just a lad, I worked for one of the best trainers in

England. He knew more about horses than anyone I've ever met, before or since. He had a young filly run a great race one afternoon. She either won it or came in second. I can't remember. When they went to see to her the next morning, there was a foal at her side. It was standing up and nursing just as bright as you please. It took some time for him to live that one down, you can be sure."

"You mean the filly was racing fit and still the foal didn't show?" said Ginny. "Oh, come on, Michael, that's hard to believe!"

"Any harder to believe than that a pony you've cared for all these months has kept her foal a secret from you?" asked Michael.

"I see what you mean," Ginny said.

"I can name two ponies in the show ring today that were just as big a surprise to their owners when they were born. One is a show hunter and one is a jumper," said Michael. "Sometimes a dealer will breed a flighty mare to settle her down. Then he'll sell her quickly without telling anyone what's been done. Sometimes the breedings are an accident. A fence gets broken down. Or a stall door is left open at the wrong time. The mare or the stud gets loose. The boy in charge of the horses sends them back to their stalls. And who's the wiser? He's not going to admit he was careless and risk losing his job."

"Were there any stallions at that awful place where you got Mokey?" asked Pam.

"Oh, sure," said Ginny. "There was at least one. A chestnut, with a lovely head and a narrow white blaze. He nearly bit Mr. Dobbs, which would have served him right. There might have been some others, too. Mr. Dobbs didn't say."

"Well, there you are," said Michael. "Not really such a surprise, is it? A man like that doesn't care one way or another about his ponies. He probably turned them all out together without a second thought. Ask your vet, Miss Ginny. He'll tell you this kind of thing happens all the time."

Dr. Nichols agreed with Michael. He stopped by a few days later. He had a vitamin-mineral supplement for Ginny to give Mokey in her feed.

"But it still seems kind of unreal," said Ginny.

"Don't put Mokey's blanket on tonight before you feed her," Dr. Nichols said. "Very often you can see the foal kick when the mother drinks water or eats her grain. A blanket would hide this. Put your hand on her flank, if you want to be sure. You can feel the foal move, even if you can't see it."

Ginny fed Mokey early that evening. Mokey stuck her muzzle into the fresh grain. Ginny felt a little foolish. But she put the palm of her hand on Mokey's flank, just in front of the pony's hind leg. Just like the doctor had told her to do.

She felt a sudden flutter under her hand. She jumped back as though she'd been stung. Feeling even more foolish, she put her hand back on the pony's flank again. This time she held it there. The flutter ended in two strong bumps against her hand. Then it stopped.

Mokey turned her head to look at Ginny. Ginny looked back at the pony in a haze of delight.

"It's real," said Ginny. "I felt it, I really did. It's true." Mokey sneezed and went back to her grain. Ginny went to get the blanket. Then she stopped to give her pony a hug. She pressed her face into the white shaggy mane. The sun set behind the ridge. The stall filled with twilight shadows. Mokey finished her grain and turned to her hay.

Ginny gave Mokey a final hug. "I don't even care whether it's a colt or a filly, or how many silly spots it has," Ginny said. She finished buckling the blanket into place. "But, Mokey, it would be nice if its eyes matched!"

# Chapter Nine

As the first weeks of early spring went by, the frozen ground began to thaw. The icy ruts of the lanes and paths turned into deep and heavy mud. The red sleigh was put back in the old hay barn. The silver sleigh bells were taken from the harness. They were polished one last time. Then they were stored away in their gray flannel bag.

The days grew longer and warmer. Ginny heard the call of mourning doves when she fed Mokey in the mornings before she left for school. Snowdrops bloomed in the sunny corner beside the kitchen steps.

Ginny rode over to Pam's one day and

the blacksmith took Mokey's shoes off. He trimmed her feet. Then he tossed the shoes into the back of his truck.

"Good little mare," he said to Mokey. "Had us all fooled, didn't you?" Mokey closed her eyes dreamily. The blacksmith and Michael traded stories about surprise foals.

"Are you sure it's okay for her not to wear shoes?" Ginny asked the blacksmith. Michael went to bring Firefly from his stall.

"The vet says she's getting near her time, doesn't he?" said the blacksmith. "Then no more shoes for a while. An unshod hoof does a lot less damage if a mare steps on her foal by accident."

Ginny shuddered. She watched while the restless Firefly was shod. He was then turned out into a white-fenced paddock to buck and play in the light spring wind.

"I'm glad I'm not on him today," Pam said. "He gets higher than a kite when the wind blows like this." She and Ginny walked back to the stable. Mokey trailed along behind at the end of the reins. "How much longer can you ride Mokey?"

"Dr. Nichols says she should be exercised," said Ginny. She looked back at Mokey with doubt. "But she's getting really big. Maybe she's going to have twins."

"Can horses have twins?" asked Pam.

"I think so," said Ginny. "Let's ask Michael."

Michael said that horses and ponies could indeed have twins, but that it didn't happen very often. It was rare for twins to live.

"One's enough," said Ginny, making a face. "I just wish it would hurry up and come. All this waiting makes me nervous."

"I don't really understand what all the fuss is about, anyway," said Pam. "Ponies have foals all the time. But this one is pretty special, I guess, because it's Mokey's."

"There you are," said Michael. "That's it exactly. Everything looks different when you come down to each mare."

Ginny looked upset. Her eyes filled with tears. "I wish all this had never happened," she said in a shaking voice. "It seemed so wonderful at first. But now I'm scared. What if something goes wrong?"

"Wild ponies have foals all by themselves, without anybody around to help," said Pam.

"That's true," said Michael. "But some of those mares die. And some of those foals as well. It may not matter in the long run to the survival of a wild herd. But it can matter a lot when it's one Thoroughbred broodmare that is foaling what may be the future winner of the Derby. Or when it's your own pony having her foal."

Ginny nodded. She was speechless.

"It would be wrong for me to say that you shouldn't worry," said Michael. "A little constructive worry never did any harm. Chances are, nine times out of ten, Mokey won't have a bit of trouble. But the thing to do is keep an eye on her. Call the vet when she first goes into labor. The foal will probably be born before he even gets there. But if the mare's in any trouble at all, he'll be there in plenty of time to help."

Ginny sniffed. She felt a little better. "I was starting to feel sort of stupid," she said. "Everybody keeps telling me I'm making too big a thing of this."

"I never told you that," said Michael. "And neither did Dr. Nichols, I don't think."

"That's true," Ginny said. "He's told me all kinds of things to do and not to do. But he's never said I could just forget about it."

She wiggled up onto Mokey's back. She pushed a stray lock of the pony's white mane over onto the right side. She waved good-bye and started the ride home. The bridle paths were so muddy that Ginny went home on the road instead. Mokey's bare hooves made a soft, pattering sound. She walked quietly

along the side of the road. A motorcycle went
by with a shattering roar. It trailed a thick blue
plume of smoke. Mokey shook her head and
shied a little.

"It's a good thing you're not like Firefly,"
Ginny said to her pony with a giggle. "You're
so round right now I can barely stay on you at
a walk!"

A few days later, Ginny opened the stall door
that led out into the paddock. Mokey came out

with her head and tail in the air. She trotted lightly across the muddy ground. Ginny stared at her. She was confused for a moment. Then she peered into the stall.

Dr. Nichols had told her that the pony was not yet ready to foal. But maybe he'd made a mistake. Maybe Mokey had fooled all of them again. Ginny felt a guilty flash of relief. She wanted to see the foal born. But it would be wonderful to have all the waiting and worry-ing over and done with.

She looked carefully in every corner. But there was no spotted little foal curled up anywhere in the stall.

She went outside to look at Mokey again. She couldn't understand it. Mokey had been moving so heavily for the past few weeks. Now she was trotting around almost like her old self. But she was still huge and round. As Ginny fed the pony, she could see the foal moving and kicking.

Puzzled, she called Dr. Nichols. "That's fine," he said. "We're making progress. The foal has changed position. It's moving down. Mokey feels less pressure. It's getting ready to be born."

"But I've got to go to school today!" Ginny said with a wail. "Will it be born today?"

"Today, tomorrow, or three weeks from now," Dr. Nichols said cheerfully. "It still may be quite a while. Tell your mother to let me know if she thinks she needs me at any time."

It was agony to get on the school bus that morning. Ginny's mother had promised she would not leave the house. She said she would check Mokey every hour through the day until Ginny got home from school. This helped a little. But Ginny had an awful day. She called home at recess and at lunch. Her mother told her that Mokey was just napping quietly in the sun in front of her stall as she always did at noon.

By the time Ginny got home that afternoon, she was frantic and out of breath. She had run all the way from the bus. But nothing had happened. Mokey was just as fat and cheerful as ever.

"I'll go get some work done," said Mrs. Anderson to Ginny as she came into the house. "Now you're here to keep an eye on things. We're all going to have to change our schedules for a while, I can see that! It won't be long. I don't want to miss the big day either!"

# Chapter Ten

The last few days of school dragged by very slowly. Then spring vacation started at last.

"It's just as well," Ginny whispered to Pam that night. "I can't remember one single thing I've read in the last two weeks. Except the foaling chapters in the vet books I got from the library."

Pam just mumbled a sleepy answer. She had come to spend the whole vacation with Ginny. That way she could be there to see the foal born. She was almost asleep in the other bed in Ginny's room. Restlessly Ginny slipped out of bed and went to the window.

It was very late. The night was crisp and cold. Ginny pulled on her bathrobe and tip-toed downstairs. She slipped her bare feet into her fleece-lined boots. She put her ski jacket on over her bathrobe. Then she made her way down to the stable.

Mokey had been clipped. But she could not wear her blanket this close to her foaling time. Dr. Nichols had told Ginny's father to hang a few heat lamps high on the walls of the stall. The soft red glow from the lamps spilled out of the window. It had looked kind of spooky at first, almost as though the stall were on fire. But everyone soon got used to it. The lights kept Mokey warm.

Ginny looked through the window into the stall. She tried not to disturb her pony. The heat lamps gave enough light for her to see that Mokey was lying down. She looked as though she were sound asleep. But the pony heard Ginny. She always did. She got to her feet. She stretched. She yawned. Then she came over to the window. She pressed her muzzle against the wire mesh that protected her from the glass.

All was well. Ginny said a soft "Good night, Moke" and went back up to the house.

"I don't see how anybody survives all this," Ginny said crossly a few days later. "Mokey's going to foal at any moment. Pam and I are taking turns getting up every two hours all night, every night. Neither of us feels as though we've slept for a month. It all seems hard to believe. The waiting is terrible."

Michael had come over to see how things were going. He clucked with understanding.

"I can share the night watch," said Mrs. Anderson.

Ginny sighed. "Thanks anyway. But Pam and I can do it. It can't be too much longer."

"That's what you said a week ago," said Pam. She was sitting on an overturned bucket by the feed room door. Her chin was in her hands. Her eyes were shut. "Why don't we just skip one night and catch up on our sleep?"

Michael grinned. "If you do, I can promise Mokey will foal that very night."

"It seems so strange that anything as big as a pony can go into labor without any warning signs at all," said Mrs. Anderson.

"It does indeed," agreed Michael. "On the big breeding farms, they watch the mares day and night in the foaling barns. But even there, many foals have been born when the night watchman just slipped out for a few minutes for a cup of coffee."

"It doesn't always happen that fast, though, does it?" asked Pam.

"Not always," said Michael. "Just often enough."

Pam yawned. "Mokey is smart enough to take naps," said Ginny's mother. "I think you two girls should follow her example. I'll take the watch this afternoon."

"I think Mokey's made the whole thing up," muttered Ginny. "I think she's just enjoying the whole thing as a joke." Mokey wandered back into her stall to eat more of her straw bedding.

Ginny and Pam slept all afternoon. They felt much better that evening. They cleaned the stall and fed Mokey. While Mokey was eating, Ginny peered hopefully at the pony's swollen udder.

"She's got milk, I'm sure," Ginny reported to Pam. She patted Mokey on the shoulder. "You've kept us waiting long enough," she said firmly. "Vacation is almost over. Have it tonight."

Mokey turned her head. She slobbered bran mash on Ginny's shoulder. She got one of Ginny's braids full of wet bran as well.

Sighing, Ginny plodded up to the house to wash her hair.

\*   \*   \*

But by Sunday evening Mokey still had not foaled. Almost in tears, Pam had to go home. School started the next morning.

"I could scream," Ginny told her mother between clenched teeth. She dragged her math book out from under her vet book and made a face. "How can I focus on this stuff all day at school? It isn't fair!"

Ginny's mother and father were understanding but firm. School came first. Anyway, the chances were that the pony would foal at night, when Ginny was home. Dr. Nichols and Michael and the vet book all said so. They couldn't be sure, of course.

Ginny knew all this. But it didn't help at all. On Monday morning, it was all she could do to drag herself out of bed, feed Mokey, and start her own breakfast. The cereal tasted soggy and stale. She pushed it aside and drank her milk. She shuddered. It tasted heavy and sour.

Ginny's mother hurried out the door. She gave her daughter a quick kiss. She promised that she would be back in less than an hour so that she could watch Mokey for the rest of the day.

Ginny got her books together. She looked at the clock on the kitchen wall. Almost time to leave for the bus. She searched in the pocket of her jacket for her gloves. Then she remembered that she'd left them in the stable that morning. They were on top of the oat bin.

With a sigh, Ginny walked tiredly down to the barn.

Mokey was still eating her breakfast. She rattled her feed tub cheerfully. Ginny poked her head through the door to say good-bye. For the hundredth time that morning, Ginny looked her pony over for any sign of coming labor. The muscles on either side of the tail sometimes showed to give warning. Or a waxy substance sometimes showed that the first milk was ready.

Nothing. Ginny sighed and turned away.

As she started to close the door, she saw Mokey raise her head. It was as though she were listening to a faraway sound. Then the pony turned. She circled once in her straw bed and quietly lay down.

Ginny stood still at the stall door. She was stunned by surprise. Mokey never left her feed until every last grain had been finished. She never lay down during the day. Except for the nap she took at noon outside her stall door when the sun was high.

Mokey got up. She pawed the straw uneasily. Then she circled the stall and lay down again.

Ginny's hands were shaking with excitement. She shut the door. She hurried outside to shut the doors leading into the paddock. Then she raced up to the house.

She flung her books on the floor. She dove for the telephone in the hall. Dr. Nichols's receptionist answered the phone. The doctor was in surgery, she said. He could not come to the telephone. Could she take a message?

"Tell him that I think Mokey's in labor!" Ginny said. She was frantic.

There was a silence that seemed to last forever. Then the receptionist's cool voice said, "Dr. Nichols will be there just as soon as he can."

Even through her excitement, Ginny understood that the doctor could not leave another animal in the middle of an operation. In a hurry, she dialed the number of the Jennings stable. Pam had already left for school. The boy who often came to help Michael with the horses answered the stable phone. He reported that Michael was out exercising Mr. Jennings's hunter. He promised to give him the message about Mokey as soon as he came in.

Ginny hesitated. She grabbed a pad and

pencil from beside the phone. She scribbled the word "Mokey" on it. She propped it against the sugar bowl on the kitchen table. This way her mother would see it as soon as she got home. Then she ran back down to the stable.

# Chapter Eleven

Mokey whinnied loudly at the sound of Ginny's footsteps. Ginny opened the door to the stall. She found the pony was up on her feet. She looked bright and carefree.

Ginny glared at Mokey with anger. "What a dirty trick," she said in a shaking voice. "You've made me miss the school bus for nothing at all. Nobody's going to believe for one minute that I really thought you were in labor."

Ginny stopped. She had been so surprised and disappointed to find Mokey standing up. Then she had been so worried about what her parents and teachers were going to say. She hadn't noticed the fresh light sweat on the pony's flanks.

"Oh, Moke," Ginny said softly. "You've got me in such a spin over this whole thing that I can't think straight. It is time now, isn't it?"

Mokey made a soft, whuffling sound. She poked her nose against Ginny's jacket and turned away. Ginny watched in silence. The pony moved restlessly around in her stall. She pawed at the straw.

Ginny forced herself to move slowly. She took a long, shivery breath. The uncertainty had gone away. Instead, Ginny felt a strange calmness. It was like the hushed stillness before a thunderstorm. She wished there were someone with her. But it couldn't be helped. She was alone with Mokey. The foal was coming. There was nothing more she could do but wait.

She sat down on the fresh pile of hay in the corner of the stall. Mokey switched her tail. She poked her side uneasily with her muzzle.

Then she lay down. A ripple of muscles moved across her flanks. The first contractions had started.

The contractions grew stronger. Mokey lay with her legs curled under her. She rested for a few minutes. Her head was outstretched. There was a dreamy, faraway look in her eyes. Ginny moved a little to ease a cramp in one leg. Mokey's eyes flew open. She turned her head to look at Ginny. Then she struggled to her feet.

Ginny murmured soothing, meaningless words. A dog barked somewhere. Mokey spun around. She was tense with fright. Ginny got up and shut the stall window. She went on talking to her pony. Mokey began to lose her look of alarm. Slowly she relaxed. She circled her stall and lay down again.

Ginny's mouth felt sandy and dry. She swallowed with a gulp. She tried to feel the calm she'd felt a few minutes before. But it was no use. She'd heard or read so many stories about mares in trouble foaling. They spun through her mind. She felt sick. She wanted to run out of the stall. She wanted to call Dr. Nichols again, or Michael, or someone. Ginny had never felt so alone in her life.

She stood at the side of the stall. She jammed her sweaty hands into her pockets. Mokey let her breath out with a soft puff from the force of a contraction. Ginny's heart jumped with a sudden rush of excitement. She could see the tip of one tiny hoof. Then there was another. One more contraction. There was the tip of a small muzzle. It looked blurred and out of focus behind the covering membrane.

"If you can see two front hooves and the muzzle of the foal, you will know its position is good." Ginny remembered Dr. Nichols telling her this. More contractions came. The foal's entire head and neck were showing. Mokey rested again.

Ginny couldn't believe it. Somehow she had thought that once the foal started to be born, all of it would come in a rush. But nothing was happening. Everything was still. There was such silence in the stall. Ginny could hear nothing but the pounding of her own heart.

The contractions started again. Mokey was breathing hard. Ginny's knees were starting to shake. She knelt in the straw beside the pony. She tried to remember some of the things she'd been told. "Don't get in the way. Let nature take its course. Don't bother the mare unless you have to." But what was the difference between getting in the way and helping? Where did one change into the other? Ginny felt tears running down her cheeks. She didn't know what to do.

She heard the door opening quietly behind her. Then Michael's low voice filled the stall with warm, comforting sounds. It drove away the awful silence that had seemed so scary. Through her tears, Ginny began to giggle. Michael's voice had the same tone she used herself when Mokey was afraid.

"Time to lend a hand," said Michael. He came calmly into the stall.

Ginny stood up. She felt dizzy with relief. "I don't know when I've been so glad to see someone," she said. Her voice was a hoarse whisper. She moved away from Mokey.

The pony turned her head. She nickered softly to Michael. Then another strong contraction took her breath away. Ginny waited for Michael to move forward. When he didn't, she looked up at him with a puzzled frown.

"Aren't you going to do something?" she said.

Michael looked back at her. "Wouldn't you like to do it yourself? You can't learn any younger," he said.

Ginny looked at Mokey for one confused moment. She paused. Then she knelt again beside the half-born foal.

"Okay," she said. "Tell me what to do."

She heard Michael's voice. It sounded as though it were coming from a long way off.

But it was clear and quiet. "The foal doesn't seem to be in trouble yet. Neither does the mare. But what you're going to do now is just help things along a little. Somewhere along the way, the foal stops getting air through the umbilical cord. Right now he's between one world and the next. Take hold of his forelegs. Then pull when the next contraction comes."

Ginny's hands were shaking. She didn't know what to expect. The membrane around the foal looked strange and slimy. Ginny had to make herself reach out. She was surprised and relieved. The legs of the unborn foal were strong and thin. They felt warm and alive in her hands.

The next contraction came.

"Good," said Michael. "Pull firmly. Down toward the mare's hocks." The foal didn't move. Mokey rested.

Ginny braced herself. With the next contraction, she gave another pull. The foal slipped gently out onto the straw.

Ginny sat back on her heels. She stared at the bundle of head and body and legs. It was lying still in its membrane covering.

"Quickly now," said Michael sharply. "Break the membrane at its head."

Ginny tugged gently at the membrane. It looked so fragile. She was shocked at how strong it was. She yanked at it with frantic fingers. It tore silently. Ginny pulled it away from the foal's tiny muzzle. Its head looked strange as it came out of its covering. Its eyes were shut. Its thin ears were limp.

Michael handed Ginny a stack of folded towels. They had been ready on the shelf in the tack room. Ginny rubbed the foal's wet head. She wiped out its nostrils.

The foal didn't move. It lay in a still, soggy heap on the straw. It didn't show the smallest flicker of life.

"It's dead!" Ginny said in a thin, shaky voice.

"Rub its sides," said Michael. He pulled the membrane back. "Hard. Don't worry. It's not as fragile as it looks." Ginny grabbed a fresh towel. She began to rub the foal's narrow body briskly.

"Breathe," she whispered. She pressed more weight on the thin little ribs. She rubbed the wet flanks harder and harder with the rough towel.

"All right," said Michael. Ginny stopped. She looked up at him with a blank face. Then she turned her head to see why he was smiling. The foal's funny little head was raised all the way off the straw. It was blinking at her from blurry eyes. It looked as though it was waking up from a long, deep sleep.

"Well, hi," said Ginny. She was sitting back on her heels. The foal sneezed. Its head fell back onto the straw.

"Fantastic," said Ginny. She was kneeling beside the foal. She watched its flanks fluttering. They moved more and more steadily as its breathing grew stronger.

"Very nice," said Michael. His thin face split in a wide grin.

Ginny went on drying the foal, more gently. Her mind stopped spinning. The rest of the stall came slowly back into focus. Mokey was lying very still, just as she'd been when the foal was born. She was breathing gently. She had a strange, faraway look in her eyes. It was almost as though she were in a trance.

"Is she okay?" Ginny asked Michael. She was worried. Michael nodded.

"Just let her alone. She's resting," he said.

The foal made a sudden effort. It put out one thin foreleg. Then it rolled to an upright position. Ginny smiled at it with pride. Slowly she began to see what she'd been far too busy to notice before. She almost didn't believe it. The foal was not spotted in uneven patches like its mother. It wasn't spotted at

all. It was a solid, rich brown. And it had a blazing white star on its forehead.

"Shouldn't I be doing something?" Ginny asked Michael. "What about the umbilical cord? Shouldn't it be cut?"

"Let it be," said Michael. "It will break when the mare gets up."

Mokey turned her head slowly. She pricked her ears. Then she gave a soft, mur-muring sound, deep in her throat. To Ginny's surprise, the foal answered with a shaky whinny.

Mokey rose to her feet. She turned to peer at her newborn foal. She was wary. Ginny moved to the side of the stall so she wouldn't be in the way. Mokey snuffled. She blew at the damp little creature lying in her straw. It was clear that she was puzzled and unsure. She put back her ears and stamped her foot.

The foal's heavy head bobbed and weaved at the end of its short neck. Mokey reached out to nuzzle its shoulder. Then she gave it a gentle nudge with her muzzle. The foal tipped over onto its side. Mokey jumped back in fright.

"Dumb pony," Ginny said. "Doesn't she know her own baby? Why is she acting like this?"

"Just give her a chance," said Michael. "All this is new to her." He got Mokey's halter and handed it to Ginny. "Put this on her. Hold her for a minute. Talk to her and pat her and let her know that everything is all right."

The foal gave another squeaky whinny. It struggled halfway to its feet. Mokey jerked the halter out of Ginny's hands. She flew to the far side of the stall. Michael brought a lead rope. Ginny got hold of her pony. The foal fell in a tangled heap with a sad little squeal.

Ginny looked at Michael. She was worried. But he seemed totally at ease. He was whistling softly under his breath. He brought the bottle of iodine from the shelf in the tack room. He soaked a piece of cotton in it. Then he pressed it against the stump of the umbilical cord on the foal's stomach.

"It's a colt," he said to Ginny over his shoulder.

Mokey snorted at the sharp smell of the iodine. The foal tried to stand up again. This time he almost made it before he fell.

"He's going to hurt himself!" said Ginny.

Michael smiled and shook his head. Ginny held Mokey. She stroked her shoulder gently with one hand. They all watched in silence as the colt rested and then tried once more to stand up.

# Chapter Twelve

Five minutes later, the colt was standing on all four legs. He was swaying from side to side.

"Great," Ginny said with pride. The colt took a single tottering step. Then he fell again. Mokey jumped and squealed and stamped her foot.

"Oh, cut it out, Mokey!" Ginny said. "What kind of a mother are you, anyway?"

Mokey stopped, looking sour.

"She doesn't really understand yet," said Michael. "She's confused and a little bit frightened. This is her first foal. Give her a chance to get used to the idea."

The colt scrambled to his feet. He walked

shakily toward his mother. Mokey's eyes grew wider. She backed away. She was nervous.

"How long can he wait?" Ginny asked. She was struggling to hold Mokey still. "Isn't he hungry? Is Mokey going to hurt him if he tries to nurse?"

"She might just now, if we weren't here," said Michael. "But we're not going to let that happen. That's enough foolishness, Mokey. Like it or not, this little fellow is your responsibility."

He scooped the staggering little foal up in his arms.

"Hold her with one hand. Pick her foreleg up with the other," Michael said to Ginny. After a short struggle, Ginny was able to do as she had been told. Michael carried the colt over to Mokey's side. He steadied the colt gently. The colt groped blindly for his milk.

Mokey squealed and switched her tail uneasily when the colt started to nurse.

"Is she trying to kick?" asked Ginny.

"She might if she could. But she can't while you're holding her foreleg up," said Michael.

The colt nursed clumsily at first. Michael held him patiently. The colt struggled to control all four of his legs and his first tries at nursing at the same time. It was difficult. More than once he started to tip over and fall. But Michael's quiet hands were there to steady him. Ginny held Mokey still.

Slowly the foal grew stronger and more sure of himself. Mokey seemed less tense and scared. Michael nodded. Ginny let Mokey's foreleg down gently. The pony turned her head. She softly nuzzled the flanks of her foal.

The colt stopped nursing. His legs buckled. He swung his head away from his mother. There were white drops of milk all over his small muzzle. His large, dark eyes were half closed. His white-starred head swayed weakly from side to side.

"What's the matter with him?" asked Ginny in a panic.

Michael smiled. "He's sleepy," he said. He eased the foal down onto the straw.

Mokey was stiff-legged. She made a circle around the stall. Then she put her head down to sniff the foal from head to tail. Almost shyly, she put out her tongue and licked his shoulder.

"She's getting braver," Ginny whispered. Mokey blew softly through flared nostrils. The foal lifted his head and nickered. He was drowsy. Then he fell asleep. Mokey nudged him with her muzzle and jumped back. The foal didn't move.

With a huge sigh, Mokey stood quietly over her foal. Her head dropped. Her muzzle was almost touching his shoulder. Then her eyes closed.

The foal was still damp. He was starting to shiver. Ginny tiptoed into the tack room and turned on the heat lamps. They bathed the sleeping foal in a pool of warm light.

"Take Mokey's halter off," Michael told Ginny in a low voice. "It's risky leaving a halter on a mare with a foal. There's always the chance of his getting a foreleg caught in it."

Shivering at the very thought, Ginny moved quietly into the stall. She slipped Mokey's halter off. Then she looked down with weary pride at the foal in the straw.

"Let them rest," said Michael. Ginny left the stall. She gently pulled the door almost shut behind her. She left it open just enough for them to watch.

Twenty minutes later, the foal woke up. He stretched. He scrambled strongly to his feet. Ginny started into the stall with Mokey's halter, but Michael waved for her to wait.

The colt teetered around his mother. Mokey stood still. She watched him. She was nervous. But she didn't move. The colt butted his small head in annoyance against her flank. He was searching for his milk. Mokey squealed softly but didn't kick. In a moment the foal was busy nursing. His short, curly tail was whisking from side to side.

As the minutes passed, Mokey lost her worried look. She turned her head. She nuzzled the nursing foal's hindquarters with a tender, loving gesture.

Ginny hadn't realized she'd been holding her breath. She let it out with a long sigh of relief.

"I guess she knows it's hers now," she said.

Michael was watching with warm approval.

"No doubt about it. She's accepted him as her own. And that's a nice colt, Miss Ginny. He's going to be well worth raising. Too bad we don't know the breeding of the sire. There's real quality there."

Ginny squinted her eyes in thought. She nodded and then laughed.

"I guess you're right," she said. "But I think he's beautiful just because he's here."

Mrs. Anderson came home. She was very disappointed to hear she'd missed the birth. Dr. Nichols came soon after. He spun into the driveway looking worried and anxious. Ginny told him quickly that everything was all right. They all went quietly down to the stable together.

Mokey didn't like having them there. She swung herself right between the open doorway and her foal. She was hiding him from sight.

"Now what's the matter with her?" Ginny said with anger. "First she won't let him near her. Now she won't let us see him!"

Michael and Dr. Nichols agreed that none of this was strange at all. Especially in a mare with her first foal. Ginny put a halter on Mokey. She held her tightly while the doctor checked the foal. Dr. Nichols gave him a tetanus and antibiotic shot. Michael held him. Then they watched as the little colt ran across the stall, back to his frantic mother.

"She'll settle down in a few days," the doctor told Ginny. "You can let them outside in the paddock for a few minutes tomorrow, if the weather's warm."

When everyone had left a few minutes later, Ginny gave the stall a good cleaning. She filled Mokey's bucket with fresh water. She emptied the uneaten grain from her feed tub. Then she went to make the pony a fresh hot mash as Dr. Nichols had told her to do.

She glanced at her watch as she made her way up to the house. It was barely noon. It seemed impossible. After all those dreary, endless weeks of waiting. All those sleepless nights and tiresome days. Now everything had happened and was over in such a short time.

She sat down for a minute on the kitchen steps. She was going over in her mind all the instructions Dr. Nichols had given her. The white snowdrops were gone from the corner beside the steps. Yellow and purple crocuses bloomed in their place. In the hazy light of the spring sun, she could see the buds of the blossoms on the apple tree next to the kitchen window. They were starting to swell and turn pink. Ginny chewed thoughtfully on the end of one braid. Spring was everywhere now. It had been almost a year since Mokey had come.

Ginny closed her eyes dreamily. What should she name the new foal? She pictured the sturdy little red-bay colt with his pretty head and blazing white star. Maybe she should call him Starlight.

A bird flew down. It hopped busily across the lawn under the apple tree. Ginny watched it for a moment. She wanted a spring name for Mokey's new foal.

Ginny stood up. The bird flew away. Its red breast flashed over the soft green of the new spring grass.

"I'm going to call him Robin," Ginny said out loud. In a daze of happy weariness, she went into the house to cut up some carrots for Mokey's mash.

# About the Author

**Jean Slaughter Doty** wrote fourteen children's books, including *Can I Get There by Candlelight?*, *The Crumb*, *The Monday Horses*, and *Summer Pony*, the companion to *Winter Pony*. In her spare time, she bred Welsh ponies, showed hunters, foxhunted, and judged equitation and pony classes at major shows, including the National Horse Show. Her stories about horses and ponies have been treasured by generations of riders—and readers—everywhere.

# About the Illustrator

**Ruth Sanderson** has illustrated over seventy books for children since 1975. She is well known for her lavishly illustrated fairy-tale picture books. In 2003, she won the Texas Bluebonnet Award for *The Golden Mare, the Firebird, and the Magic Ring*. Earlier in her career, she illustrated the first paperback covers for the entire Black Stallion series, as well as a number of chapter-book horse stories. She lives with her family in Easthampton, Massachusetts, and her favorite hobby is horseback riding. Visit her on the Web at www.ruthsanderson.com.

To find out how Ginny and Mokey met,
read the companion novel *Summer Pony*,
also by Jean Slaughter Doty.

Turn the page for an excerpt!

# Summer Pony

by Jean Slaughter Doty

"Why, she's blind in one eye!" gasped Ginny.

"No, miss, she's not blind. She's got one brown eye and one blue one. Just because they don't match doesn't mean she can't see perfectly well. Makes her look a bit special, don't you think? Come on, then, up you go!" Before Ginny knew what was happening, he had boosted her up onto the pony's thin bare back. He put the reins into her hands. "Off you go and give her a try. Enjoy yourself."

Ginny glanced at her mother. She was smiling. "You look very nice on her, dear," she said. Ginny smiled back. But her face felt stiff, as though the smile would crack it. She turned her attention to the thin pony under her. "Come on, you poor creature," she said under her breath. "Let's get this over with."

*If you like books about animals, you might also want to read . . .*

# For anyone who has ever dreamed of hearing a horse's story...

# Ghost Horse

by George Edward Stanley

Emily got out of bed. She ran to the window and pulled back the curtains. In the moonlight, she could see the beautiful white horse!

Emily pinched herself. "Ouch!" Now she knew she wasn't dreaming. The beautiful white horse was really there!

He started walking toward her window. But the closer he got, the paler he got.

Emily gasped. She could see through the horse!

"You're . . . you're a ghost!" she whispered.

# SILVER

## by Gloria Whelan

Right on my tenth birthday and just two days before Dad was to leave for the Iditarod, Ruff had five puppies. "Because they were born on your birthday," Dad said, "I'll give you one of the puppies—the runt of the litter. He probably won't make much of a racing dog."

My pup had one blue eye and one brown eye. He had soft, downy fur the color of shiny coins. "I'm going to call him Silver," I said.

# White Bird

## by Clyde Robert Bulla

When John Thomas was tired of staying inside,
he went out into the rain. He found that he
could walk in the woods and keep almost dry.
The branches were like a roof over his head.

One morning after a storm, he went to the
woods. He came upon a great oak that had been
struck by lightning. The trunk was split and
burned. At the foot of the tree was something
white.

At first he thought it was a flower or a toad-
stool. Then he saw it was a bird.